PIPER HERBERT

THE LAST CHANCE

AANYA JHAVER

Made with ♥ on the Notion Press Platform
www.notionpress.com

Thank you to my family for inspiring me to pursue my passion. Their endless love, support, and encouragement have been my source of strength throughout this journey.

A special thanks to my 'Badi Nani' (Great Grand Mother) and 'Nanu' (Grandpa), who played a great part in my love for reading. They always believed that i could and would write my own book some day.

A special thanks to 'Bunty Mama' (Uncle) for doing the proof reading.

A special thanks to Nani(Grandma), my parents and family members who have always been positive and motivated me.

A special thanks to Shonali Ma'am who always appreciated my diary entries and letters in school, which inspired me to write further.

Lastly, a very special thanks to 2 of my friends, who were very supportive the whole time.

Love

Aanya

Contents

Preface

Dear Reader,

My name is Aanya, and I'm excited to share with you my first book. As a 12-year-old, I've always loved reading books about adventure, fantasy, and mystery. These tales have taken me to faraway lands and allowed me to experience things that I thought were impossible.

I've also always loved writing. I remember writing short stories and poems sharing them with my family and friends.

This book tells the story of a girl, a 15-year-old who is assigned to investigate a powerful gang run by other teens. As she navigates through the ups and downs of life, she learns valuable lessons about courage, friendship, and determination.

Writing this book has been a journey of self-discovery. Through Piper's experiences, I was able to explore my own beliefs and values. I hope that reading this book will take you on a journey of your own and inspire you to face your challenges head-on.

Thank you

Happy Reading!

1

2 months ago:

Everything shone in the bright sun in Cannonville. The weather was warm. Children rode bikes, walked in groups and skateboarded on the road. People in their mid seventies sat in gardens and couples sat in cafes talking and laughing.

The whole town must've been outside that afternoon except for one family. The Herbert's were sitting around the kitchen table looking sad and unhappy. Especially Piper, who was trying to blink back tears.

The Herbert's were a family of six. They were, Mr John Herbert, Mrs Fanny Herbert, Charlie [who had been the eldest], James and Piper, and the youngest, Olivia. The Herbert's were a fun family. You would know that if you would just glance around the living room. The walls were lined with pictures of the family, laughing and smiling. There were souvenirs from all around the world. The sofas were comfortable and everything had a warm, happy feel to it.

Charlie had disappeared for over two years now. No one knew where he was.

The cause for their sadness was the letter that Piper held in her hand. It went like this:

Miss Piper Herbert,

I hope all is well. I am writing to ask if you would like to take up a mission. I know it hasn't been a month after the last mission, but we are desperately in need of a clever person like you. I cannot tell you the details of the mission here, in this letter for it might fall in wrong hands but I must warn you that this mission is very dangerous. You can lose your life if you are not careful. However, it is up to you, to decide whether you want to take up the mission or not.

If you accept, please contact Professor Lilly for your fake identity. You will have to leave in two days. All the necessities will be provided for. Please contact me for more details.

Kind regards,

Mr Vanhoover

Head of the Spies1991

***

Spies1991 was an organization that recruited spies from all over the world. The head was Mr Vanhoover. Now you might be wondering how could *15 year olds* leave school to go on dangerous missions that risked their lives. The children that were taken in had to go through a few 'tests' and they could only go on missions when they turned 15. Well, dangerous missions.

Mr and Mrs Herbert looked at each other, sadness clear in their eyes. They had already lost their son two years ago. 'Well John, Piper is over *15* now, so it is up to her to make a decision' Mrs Herbert said, trying to keep her voice straight.

Mr Herbert sighed. 'Fanny, we *already lost* Charlie' John Herbert said, his voice wavering slightly.

Piper looked at the letter. This mission could kill her but on the other hand could she say no?

'Mum, I'll only decide after I've talked to Mr Vanhoover' Piper said firmly.

Just as she was saying those words, the flat screen TV, flickered to life showing a man in his forties, sitting on a leather chair. Piper turned and bowed. Mr Vanhoover smiled. 'Ah, I see you've got the letter' he said.

'Mr Vanhoover, could you tell me the details of this mission?' Piper asked.

A series of news reports came on the television. A middle-aged woman with short cropped golden hair stood in front of a jewellery store. 'Diamonds worth 50 million dollars have been stolen from Diamonds4life in broad daylight' she said. Piper whistled. The screen shifted and showed a series of newspaper clippings.

FIFTY CARS STOLEN IN NEW JERSEY

10 MILLION DOLLARS WORTH RUBIES DISAPPEAR IN TEXAS

1 MILLION DOLLARS WORTH COUNTERFEIT MONEY DISCOVERED

The screen flickered and Mr Vanhoover appeared again. 'Your brother Charlie discovered all these thefts were done by a gang, based in New Jersey'. 'Was this the gang Charlie went behind and disappeared?' She asked.

Mr Vanhoover nodded grimly. Piper's mind worked fast. *If Charlie had disappeared, there was a two percent chance that he was alive. If, she got in by any chance, she could find Charlie, hand over the gang to the police and come back home safe.* 'I'm in' she blurted. She had a feeling that this mission was more than just finding a gang of criminals in New Jersey.

2

It was late in the night and Piper was walking around her room. It hadn't occurred to Piper then that she could fall to her death on that mission.

I get into that gang, I rescue Charlie and then hand over the gang to the police. It's a piece of cake, Piper said to herself.

She walked over to her desk and turned on the lamp. Her eyes fell on a framed picture that sat on the desk. It was a picture of her, James and Charlie before Charlie had disappeared and James had gone for a mission. It had been taken two years ago on their thirteenth birthday. Their faces shone with happiness. She wished she could go back to that day.

Piper stiffened as footsteps sounded outside her room. Mrs Herbert opened the door gently and looked inside. 'Didn't sleep yet?' she asked. Piper shook her head. 'Did you hear from James?' she asked. Mrs Herbert shook her head. She nodded and walked towards her bed.

'I better get some sleep' she said, climbing in. 'Good night'

***

'Let us see what we can do' Professor Lilly said as she turned Piper around in her chair.

She was sitting in a dark dressing room with dim lights.

'Uh professor? I need to look like a gangster' Piper said.

'I know what I am doing girl' Professor Lilly replied, irritated. She gritted her teeth as the professor put on a blindfold over her eyes.

Two hours later, the Piper who came out of the room wasn't the same Piper who had gone in. Her chocolate brown hair was dyed blonde and cut unevenly, her eyes which were originally brown, glowed green. She wore high heeled black boots with golden spikes that glinted dangerously, ripped black shorts and a blue shirt.

'Mr Vanhoover will be here in just about...now' Professor Lilly said, looking at her watch.

'Are you ready?' Mr Vanhoover asked, coming from yet another room right on cue. Piper turned around and bit her lip.

'I'm not sure' she said. She suddenly felt anxious.

She wasn't sure if she would succeed anymore. She couldn't back out now. Fear enveloped her heart. She could die. She looked around the room, biting her lip. Piper wanted to cry and back out but she kept a straight face.

As she got in the car that would take her to New Jersey, Mr Vanhoover handed her a fake ID. 'Piper, you will be stationed at Diamonds4life' Mr Vanhoover said, before shaking hands with her and closing the door.

The car sped downtown in silence. Piper seemed to battle with herself. How could she have said yes. She could die on this mission. Why had she been so dumb.

Piper looked at her fake ID and read the name she was supposed to go along with. Summer Mannering, the name read. She closed her eyes and leaned back.

3

The driver slipped a fake diamond into Piper's hand as she walked towards the road, her spiky heels glimmering in the sunlight. Strangers bustled about the road minding their own business.

A few shot Piper disapproving glances before walking or jogging off. She smiled sweetly at them and then crossed the road confidently, not daring to look back in case someone was watching her.

She stopped when she saw a man outside the jewellery store. She studied him carefully. He was a short man, with hair that looked like it had been electrocuted. His eyes were smeared with eyeliner, possibly to make him look scary and his lips were red like he had just smeared red lipstick all over them. Neon green nail polish covered his middle finger.

She walked in and a man with short cropped hair stood behind the counter. 'Good morning' she said.

'What are you interested in?' the man asked, eyeing Piper's boots. She smiled. She could sense the guy looking at her from outside. This was definitely one of the members in the gang.

She had to be very quick but extremely careful. 'Can you show me some stones?' she asked.

'As in rocks?' asked the man, laughing at his joke. Great. This man was also dumb. Out loud, she laughed.

'Oh no, I meant like rubies and sapphires' she said smiling brightly. She looked over the stones and shook her head. 'Do you have something more...sparkly?' she asked.

'Sure, do' the man said, pulling out a tray of diamonds.

Piper's eyes sparkled as bright as the diamonds when she saw them. They ranged in different sizes, from small to big. Her eyes fell on a diamond which was an exact replica of the one she had in her pocket.

She gripped the plastic diamond tightly. In the other hand she held the other diamond, pretending to be interested in it by turning it over and over. She looked around the shop. She needed a distraction. Fast.

She spotted a window right behind the guy and made her eyes go wide with fear and dread. 'That, that building!' she gasped, pointing behind him. 'It'sonfire!' she yelled.

The man turned and she swiftly changed the diamonds. 'Hey, there is no-' the man behind the counter said turning around but Piper was already gone. It took the man a few seconds to realise that the diamonds had been replaced.

'HEY' he yelled as he rushed outside. The guy outside with the electrocuted hair tackled him. While Piper dodged a few people and then came to a junction.

The man from the jewellery store was closing in from behind and police cars were lining on the road. Someone tried grabbing her from the back but she turned around and kicked the man. The spikes from the shoes glinted dangerously as the man fell down.

Everyone else backed off. Two police officers got out of the car and held up guns. 'Hands up mam' the first officer said. Piper was filled with dread.

This could end really really bad. Instead, she started running. The first police officer fired and Piper rolled down, dodging the bullet. She jumped on top of the police car and then jumped on a tree. She climbed it as fast as she could and then jumped on a roof of a building. Training really paid off.

The police were coming up the stairs of the building now. She had to think fast. There were rows of buildings on the road, all connected. The door burst open and the two policemen staggered in huffing and panting.

Piper was just about to jump on to the next building when the first officer shot again. She jumped and ducked as the bullet flew past her. 'See you again!' she said smiling before she ran and jumped on the third building. She looked down. There was an alleyway right under the building. Bricks stuck out here and there. Without thinking she started climbing down. The road was made with tar so if she fell down, she didn't want to think about it. She jumped the last few feet and landed on the tar road. She turned left and came to a dead end.

There were a few dumpsters on one side. She jumped in one and thankfully it was empty. She waited there for what seemed like hours. She felt dreadful for the stunt she had pulled but she couldn't undo it. All of it was a part of the mission. She shuddered to think what would happen if she had fallen down the building.

She slowly lifted the dumpster and looked out. The alley way was deserted. She got out slowly and screamed when something pounced on her, covered her mouth. The last thing she saw before blacking out was the black cloth.

When Piper woke up, she found herself tied to a chair. She tried screaming through the gag. She was utterly horrified. The guy outside the jewellery store was towering above her, grinning.

'Kate, remove her gag and let her speak' he ordered. Another girl came into view. She wore black clothes; her face was pale and her eyes were stormy grey.

Piper knew her. She racked her memory to remember where she had seen her. Her head throbbed with pain as she tried to think. The girl came forward and pulled the cloth that was tied around Piper's mouth.

If she recognised her, she didn't show any signs of it. 'Who are you?' Piper demanded, although she had a feeling that he was one of the members in the gang.

'Ever heard of the Scavengers?' the guy asked her.

'No' Piper said.

The guy showed her a few newspaper clippings. These were the same clippings Piper had seen on the screen. 'I saw your little stunt today missy' the guy said, slowly walking around Piper.

She felt a cold chill run down her spine. 'I am Ken' the guy said.

Piper laughed sarcastically. 'Ken as in Ken from Barbie?! Because you don't look the least bit handsome' she said boldly.

Ken snarled. 'Don't talk to me that way little girl' he said.

'Or what' Piper asked, her eyes narrowed. She had to appear like a bad kid who didn't care about the world.

Ken was clearly taken aback by such audacity. 'You're gonna kill me?' Piper pressed on, sneering.

'Look, I brought you here to ask if you would join the Scavengers' Ken said simply.

'We could use a person like you' he said, playing with Piper's hair.

'Don't touch my hair' Piper said through gritted teeth.

'So, do you accept or not?' he asked. 'If you do, you get to hang out with a cool guy like me' he said. Piper scoffed.

'Me hanging out with you? she said. 'Dream that in your dreams Kenny boy' she said sarcastically.

'You get your own room, get brand new clothes, good food for free and money for all the crimes you commit' Ken said, ignoring the last sentence.

'I accept' Piper said slowly, trying to hide her smile. She was in.

'What's your name?' Kate asked her, as she cut her ropes.

'Summer Mannering' Piper said.

***

Her heels made the only noise in the dark stone corridor that Kate led her through. Kate stopped in front of a room that had the number 402 written on it. 'This is your room' she said, opening the door.

'Where's your room?' Piper asked.

'Next door' Kate replied. Kate's room was the last room in the corridor.

'Can you help me unpack?' Piper asked suddenly.

Kate would know everything that went on in the Scavengers and if she could get close to Kate, she would get to know every move of the gang. ‘Sure’ Kate said, her face breaking out into a smile.

The two entered the room. It was a small bedroom. You couldn’t call it ‘comfortable’. It was furnished with a bed, a cupboard, a chair and a table and two windows. Another door, stood at one end. ‘Where does that lead to?’ Piper asked.

‘My room’ Kate replied. ‘Wait a second’ Kate said suddenly. She walked out of the room and closed the door. Piper heard Kate going inside her room and locking it. The door in Piper’s room that connected her to Kate’s room opened and Kate came in smiling.

‘Sorry, Ken doesn’t like us going into other rooms’ she said.

‘Does he know about the door?’ Piper asked. Kate shook her head and grinned.

‘He doesn’t know a lot of stuff’ she muttered under her breath. ‘Anyways’ she said out loud, ‘Lets get you unpacked!’ There wasn’t much to unpack.

Piper made a mental note to pack everything once Kate had left. ‘So, how many years have you been working here?’ she asked suddenly.

Kate stiffened and bent low, hiding her face. ‘Two years’ she said slowly. Charlie had disappeared two years ago. ‘Do you want to come out for a walk with me tomorrow?’ Kate asked.

‘Sure, I would love to’ she said.

‘Be ready by 7’ Kate answered and then shut the door. As soon as she was gone,

She lay on the bed, restless. She didn’t know when she had dozed off, but when she got up, her watch read 3:41

AM. Her phone lit up the room, illuminating the objects in the room. Piper switched off and went back to an uneasy sleep.

5

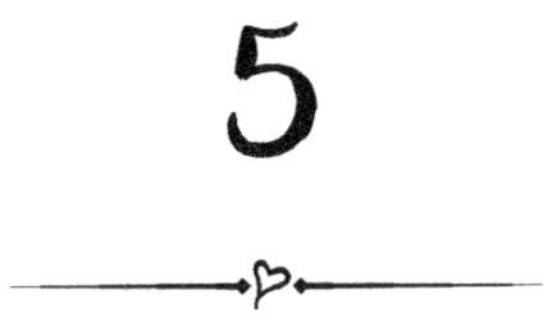

Piper sat up groggily to a knock on the door. She looked at her phone. Who was knocking at 6:21 AM?

'Who is it?' she asked, sitting up. Warm sunlight flooded the room. The door opened and Kate poked her head in. 'Good morning!' Kate said breezily, coming into the room.

Piper rubbed her eyes. 'I thought we were going out at 7' she said out loud. 'Yep, but I thought of showing you around' Kate replied, as she opened one of the windows and looked out.

Piper nodded. 'Gimme a few minutes' she said. After she had got dressed, the two set out. 'Where are we anyways?' she asked as the two set out once again on the stone corridor.

In the sunlight, Piper noticed that this wasn't any ordinary stone passage. The walls were adorned with old paintings and tapestries. They were all very dusty as if someone hadn't dusted them in a few hundred years. All the four stone corridors looked down at the quadrangle.

As Piper looked down, she caught sight of a guy about her age. He had dark brown hair but the colour of his eyes could not be determined from that distance. The balconies that stood in the corridor were all dusty.

'Do they ever clean this place?' she asked Kate, wrinkling her nose. Kate smiled. 'This mansion is located right in the heart of the woods. Most of the people consider it haunted and we do have visitors occasionally, coming to investigate this place' Kate said. 'There have been some times when helicopters have landed here, to come investigate' Kate continued. 'Ken thinks its best if we don't dust any other places apart from our rooms because it would raise suspicion if someone did come to visit again' she finished. Piper whistled. Ken was clever.

A spiral staircase led down from the corridor to a large oak door. Kate pushed it open and Piper sneezed as a cloud of dust flew around her. They were now in the quadrangle. Rows of seats lined half the place. On the front was something like a stage.

The guy whom Piper had seen came towards them. Piper could see that he had dark brown eyes, the same colour as his hair. 'Hey Kate' the boy said, ignoring Piper. Piper felt annoyed.

She liked it when people gave attention to her. That was one flaw in her nature. She wanted to dislike Kate for not introducing her but she couldn't.

Kate had a calm and easy-going nature that made people try very hard to dislike her. 'We're going for a walk then to the café. Want to join us?' Kate asked the boy. He seemed to consider it for a second and then shook his head.

'Maybe next time' he said ruefully. 'Ken's gonna kill me if I don't finish his work.' 'Cya then' Kate said as the boy walked off. Piper felt annoyed and angry. The boy had completely ignored her even though knowing the fact that she had been standing right there.

'Who is he?' Piper asked. 'Thomas. He's a good kid' Kate said, walking along. Piper scoffed and walked along. Huge rusted gates stood half open. Ivy hung from the walls. 'Follow me' Kate said once they were out of the gates. The woods twisted and turned as the two made their way through it.

Piper actually thought that they would get lost but then at last, they broke free of the woods and entered the countryside. 'Welcome to Brook Valley' Kate said.

6

Piper gaped at the landscape. They were standing on a highway surrounded by mountains powdered with snow. From the top, she could see a small, happy town. The air was cold and Piper instantly regretted not bringing her coat.

'How long is the walk from here?' Piper asked Kate. 'About 20 minutes' Kate replied, walking down. A few cars sped past dangerously. Soon they entered the town.

The town was a pretty little place. Almost like it had come from an old painting. Houses, shaped like mushrooms lay, set aback from the streets. A small grocer's shop stood around a corner. Women wearing different clothes walked about, their baskets dangling from their hands, talking and laughing. Children wearing trousers and shirts roamed around, hitting and running after one another. Men went by on cycles. It was a pretty picture.

'The people here kinda hate pollution so the whole place only has about four cars' Kate said. Piper stopped to stare at Kate. They had 3 cars at home. They walked through different streets and then entered the café, Kate had been talking about.

It was a small place with a lot of tables, there were a variety of food to choose from. Piper settled for blueberry pancakes and Kate settled for a raspberry milkshake.

'How old are you?' Piper asked her as she took a bite of her pancake. 'eighteen' Kate said. 'Why were chairs set in the quadrangle?' Piper asked suddenly. 'It's for the three tests' Kate replied. Piper raised her eyebrows. 'Every new member has to do three tests' Kate said. 'If they pass, they can stay but if they don't, they are given a pill that makes them forget their memory' finished Kate, taking a sip of her smoothie.

Piper lost her appetite. Kate grinned. 'I don't think Ken is going to do anything to you though' she said with a wink. Piper punched Kate and laughed. 'He better not' she said with a twinkle in her eye.

The door opened right then and Ken walked in with Thomas. He looked thunderous. 'Kate-' Ken started, then he saw Piper and stopped. 'Hey Summer' Ken said looking at the floor. Piper felt disgusted.

She looked at Thomas who was looking at her as if considering her. Piper still felt angry at him for ignoring her. She turned towards her pancakes and started eating.

'What happened?' Kate asked Ken. 'I told him to arrange the chairs and guess what he did?' Ken said angrily. 'What?' Kate asked. 'He went into the forbidden side of the woods' Ken finished.

Piper looked at Thomas closely. His eyes were red as if he had been crying. But why? He met her eyes and then hung his head.

But when Piper turned around she saw Kate, her face was chalk white and she seemed to be clutching a necklace. Piper decided the only way she would find out was go into the woods herself.

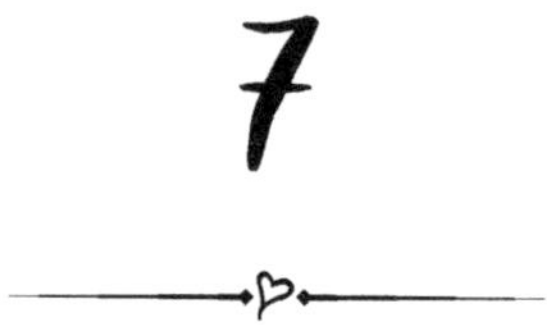

Piper knocked on Kate's room for the fifth time. No answer. It was well past 5 and Ken had said to report downstairs in about 10 minutes. Piper went into her room and opened the door that led to Kate's room.

Kate's room was about the same size as Piper's room. Her bed had been hastily made, her cupboard littered with clothes, a bookshelf crammed with books stood next to her desk and her desk itself was a mess. Papers, books, stationery and other items lay strewn across the desk. The room looked like it had never been cleaned before.

Piper looked around the room curiously but before she had time to look around, the door opened and Kate stumbled in. Her face was streaked with mud and her clothes were torn. Her eyes were red but she was smiling.

'Piper! What are you doing in my room?' Kate asked, staring at her. 'Ken's asked everyone to come downstairs in about five minutes' Piper said. 'Wait for two minutes' Kate said.

Piper came to her room and walked towards the windows, her heels tapping the floor. The view from the window was wonderful. From where she was standing, she could see miles and miles of woods.

'I see you two are late' Ken said, to Piper and Kate. 'The tests are almost half over' he said to Piper. 'I thought you told me to come down in about 10 minutes' she said. After they sat down Ken called Piper. 'You'll only have to pass one test, that is fighting' Ken said grinning. Piper nodded. She felt sick inside. 'With whom?' she asked. 'Me' Ken replied.

She got up and walked down slowly, almost majestically. Her hair blew gently and her eyes blazed as she caught the sword Ken threw at her and faced him, gritting her teeth.

She locked eyes with Thomas and then turned to face Ken. Piper and Ken circled one another. The whole crowd held their breath.

Piper slashed and Ken blocked the blow with his sword. He struck but Piper side stepped. She attacked a few more times, succeeding in gashing his hand.

Ken attacked and Piper blocked. When she suddenly figured that Ken was going easy on her because she was a girl, anger blazed inside her. She tried something she hadn't tried in a long time.

She jumped up, turned in the air, pointed the tip of the sword at Ken's throat and landed on the ground, her heels making the only sound in the whole place. The crowd went wild. Apparently, nobody had defeated Ken.

She grinned at him. 'One piece of advice Ken' she said. 'Never underestimate me' and with that she was gone. She dropped the sword on his feet and walked off, her head held high.

***

'That was great' Kate said to Piper, that night. 'I better go get some sleep' Piper said yawning. 'Good night!' Kate said and walked out. Piper waited for the cuckoo clock in her room to strike one in the morning.

Once she was sure everybody was asleep, she slowly made her way down and out of the gates hoping nobody had seen her. As soon as Piper had stepped out, 'Going somewhere?' Someone asked from behind.

8

Piper stopped in her tracks. From the corner of her eye, she knew at once that the person was Thomas. What was he doing up so late? She remained quiet.

'Why are you following me?' Asked Piper. 'Nobody goes outside at 1 AM in the morning except if they are hiding something' Thomas said. 'So either I come with you or I tell Ken' he said, walking up to her.

Piper scowled in the darkness. There was no way she could search the woods for any signs for Charlie now. 'Fine, you can come with me' said Piper, walking into the forbidden side of the woods. *There had to be something there for Ken to keep it out of bounds.*

The woods felt sinister. Trees stood there without moving, there was no moon, no sound of anything. The ground was littered with twigs.

Piper suddenly stopped at a clearing. The woods were branching into two tunnels. *Why were there tunnels in the woods?* Piper thought. Thomas stopped behind her. 'Which way now?' Piper whispered to Thomas. She had a feeling someone had been following them.

'I don't know' Thomas whispered back. Piper looked at him and noticed that he was clutching a far stick. 'Hide' he hissed suddenly.

The two of them duck behind trees just as a hooded figure made it's way to the clearing. Piper's heart raced. She knew this person. It was someone very familiar. The person wore leather shoes and a suit for some reason.

Piper thought for a minute if he had been sleepwalking. But that wasn't the case here. The person seemed to scan the place with its eyes.

How he did it with his face concealed behind a hood Piper did not know. Slowly, he made his way towards the trees, Thomas and Piper were hiding behind.

Piper panicked. Her heart throbbed with fear as the man drew closer. She could see now that it was a man. His face was hidden behind the hood but she could still catch glimpses of his face here and then.

He drew closer to the trees, growling like a dog now. Thomas was clutching the stick, ready to knock the man over. His face was pale. Piper looked up. Trees lined the whole place.

She could see trees lining the tunnel from outside. There was little space, just enough to squeeze through. She beckoned to Thomas and then started running just as the man pounced. Piper ran into the thicket as fast as she could.

She cursed herself for not wearing sneakers. Heels were not exactly the best when you're running through a thicket of trees right outside a tunnel while getting chased by a hooded man.

Piper looked back, Thomas was running as fast as he could behind her. He was trying to tell her something but he was so far and put out breath it was kind of hard to hear him. He pointed at the sky and Piper saw what he was seeing. The man was following them on air. Like he was literally FLYING in the air right above them, looking for a place to descend.

9

Piper froze in her place, Thomas right next to her. 'what are you doing' he hissed. The man would descend any moment. Piper looked at the tunnel. If they could climb on the top, they could see which direction the old mansion was located. Possibly to even see it.

The only way they could get on that was to get on top of the tunnel and the only way on top was to climb a tree and jump on top. It was a fat chance but it was also there only chance.

'Follow me' Piper yelled and started climbing the tree. Again cursing herself for not wearing sneakers. Once she was halfway up she had to time her jump carefully. The tree was now shaking with her weight.

She climbed up and finally reached the top of the tree. The tunnel was just over ten feet apart. The tree note moved dangerously. Just as it served forward Piper jumped.

She closed her eyes, preparing to fall but when she opened her eyes, she had landed on red brick. Her clothes were torn, her hair was dishevelled and blood trickled down her hands from all the scratches.

She looked down. Thomas was climbing up another tree. Unfortunately, the tree wasn't strong enough to hold him. As it started falling, Thomas jumped and caught a clump of weeds that grew from the tunnel. He looked tired.

'Thomas!' Piper said, shrilly as she ran and helped him up. 'Thanks' the boy said. Piper nodded. They were a few feet away from the mouth of the tunnel.

As they turned around though, they came face to face with the hooded man. Piper looked at Thomas. This seemed unreal. They were lost in the woods with a hooded man who could fly chasing them. It was crazy. She almost expected this to be a dream.

The girl pinched herself to make sure she wasn't dreaming and winced. 'HAH' the man said cackling as the sight of two dishevelled teenagers in ragged clothes standing on top of a tunnel at 3 AM in the morning.

'Who are-' Piper started then suddenly next to her, Thomas collapsed. Piper looked down horrified. She knelt down in front of Thomas and shook him, her eyes filled with concern.

She had only known him for one day but there was something about him that she couldn't place. Thomas was lying in a way that only the person who was in front of her could see her face.

Slowly, he opened his eyes and winked at Piper before closing them again. It dawned to Piper then that he was acting. Thomas was lying near the edge. One push and he would tumble down.

The hooded man came closer to look at Thomas. He was standing right at the edge now. The boy didn't waste a second. He sprung up and kicked the figure hard. The man, completely taken aback fell down the tunnel and into the trees below.

'Nice trick' Piper said grinning. Thomas nodded in appreciation. 'What can I say' he said grinning. 'But how did he manage to fly?' asked Thomas. 'Black magic' Piper replied, walking towards the edge of the tunnel.

Thomas looked at her as if she was crazy. 'How do you know' he asked. 'Because I am one' Piper said simply hovering over two centimetres in the air.

10

'How are you doing it?!' Thomas asked, gaping. Piper stopped flying and landed on the tunnel. 'I don't know' she said slowly, trying to hide the confusion in her voice. For the first time Thomas saw the real Summer underneath her manner.

'How do you know black magic?' he asked her. She took a deep breath. 'When I was over five, I found this diary in the attic of my house. The whole diary was filled with old spells and numbers. I memorised some of them. Watch this' she told him. She murmured something and conjured up a small fire on her palm for over two seconds. 'You need a lot of energy' she said.

Thomas gaped at her. 'Its takes a lot of practice to fly that high. Only masters in black magic can do that' Piper said. Thomas was still gaping.

'Right now, we need to get back' she said to him. 'Yes...but how?' Thomas asked, returning back to earth. 'We can't jump down, that would be suicide' Piper said. Before they could move, the tunnel started rumbling. A train was passing right under them.

Piper looked at Thomas. 'What if we get on the train and then jump down from it' Piper said suddenly. 'Jump down from a running train?!' Thomas asked. Piper nodded.

Thomas shook his head but Piper wasn't going to take no for an answer. The train was coming out now. 'On the count of three' Piper said. She wondered herself if she had gone mad. 'One, two and THREE' she said. Both of them landed on the train. Her heels clanged against the metal surface. All she would have to do was jump down.

Without any warning she slid down, Thomas caught hold of her hand just in time. 'Thomas, leave my hand' Piper shrieked in the night. 'You'll die' Thomas yelled back. 'I won't' Piper said. She tugged hard and fell right next to the railway line. Thomas slid down and crashed right on top of her.

The passengers Inside were looking at them in alarm now. 'Ow' Piper groaned. Thomas rolled next to her. 'What did you do that for' he mumbled. 'Sorry' Piper said, getting up with some effort. There wasn't any energy left in her body anymore. She wanted to lie down and sleep.

'We better get back' Thomas said, helping Piper get up. They had only known each other for a day but Piper felt she had known him her entire life. Both of them walked through the tunnel and came to the clearing.

All they had to do was follow the path they had come through. But which way? They walked on, stumbling and slipping. Finally, the old mansion came to sight. Piper almost hugged Thomas and then stopped.

'Thanks for coming with me' Piper said awkwardly. Thomas nodded and smiled. 'It was a good night' he said and then walked the other way, probably back to his room. Piper stared after him. He wasn't as bad as she had thought. He reminded her of James.

Why hadn't he contacted her? Then she realised she still hadn't found the shack Kate had a picture of. She dismissed the thoughts. She had done enough for a night.

She went up the stairs, into her room and fell on her bed, not knowing when sleep took over her.

11

Piper got up, then groaned and fell onto her bed. Every part of her body ached. She got up and managed to get ready. The clock read 10:21 AM. Shoot. She was late for breakfast. Kate had told her breakfast would start at 10.

Piper limped downstairs slowly. Her hands and legs were covered with cuts. She prayed nobody would notice. But as soon as she entered the long quadrangle where breakfast was being served Kate ran towards her.

She stopped when she saw all the cuts and scratches. 'Where have you been?' she asked her. Piper looked down. 'In bed?' she said, not quite meeting Kate's eyes. 'I sleep walk' she said shrugging.

Thomas lumbered up to them. He had a black eye and the same amount of scratches. Piper winced when she saw him. 'Good morning' he said cheerfully. 'What happened to you?!' Kate asked, looking at Thomas. 'Just banged myself' he said, as if nothing had happened.

Someone called Kate then and she disappeared, leaving both of them alone. 'I'm going into the woods again tonight' Piper said to Thomas. 'For what?' Thomas complained. 'Are you coming out not' Piper snapped. 'what time?' Thomas asked. '1 AM' she replied. 'fine' he said slowly.

As Thomas walked off, something dropped out from his back pocket. Piper ran in the front and picked it up. It was a crumpled photograph.

The photograph showed a young boy, probably Thomas with an older man probably his father. They had the same features. Both of them were standing next to a fireplace. Thomas was sitting on the man's shoulders, grinning.

It made Piper miss James even more. She searched for Thomas and saw him walking out through the garden gate. She walked towards him and then stopped abruptly.

From where Piper was standing she could see him was sitting on a tree stump, his head buried in his hands. She thought for a moment and then went up to him.

'Hey, this fell out of your pocket' she said slowly. He looked up. His eyes were red. 'Are you okay?' Piper asked, sitting down. 'Yeah just leave me alone' he said. 'Alright' Piper said getting up and throwing the photograph in front of him. 'You can have the stupid photograph'. She stalked off angrily.

***

That night, as soon as Piper was sure everyone were in bed, she crept downstairs. She would go and find the shack on her own tonight. She filled her fanny pack with necessary supplies and then quickly made her way downstairs. To her surprise, Thomas was waiting down by the gate for her.

She scowled. Why was he there? 'What are you doing here?' she asked him. 'Dint you tell me to meet you here tonight?' he answered. Piper bit her lip. 'I can handle myself' she told him. 'yea totally' Thomas replied sarcastically. With that, both of them set out into the woods.

12

The last thing both of them saw before running was Ken and the hooded figure getting up and starting after them. 'So your real name is Piper?' Thomas asked, panting as the two of them ran through the streets. 'You do know that now isn't a great time to ask me that but the answer is yes' Piper answered.

They reached the mountain and starting running faster. 'Go into the woods' Piper ordered as the woods came close with every step. Frantically they dove for the woods and hid in the cover of bushes.

It was a cloudy night and the moon wasn't up. 'Do you think they can fly?' Thomas whispered, after two minutes of silence. 'Flying takes a lot of power and energy' Piper said. 'The grandmaster would be able to do it in a few seconds but we still had a head start.

'Then why didn't he fly back up after I pushed him down the tunnel' Thomas asked. 'He was too in shock' Piper replied. They waited for a few more minutes and then a low groaning noise, like a motor, filled the air.

Piper looked at Thomas, biting her lip so hard, she thought it was bleeding.

The bush they were hiding behind didn't give them a lot of cover. 'Do you know any hiding spots?' Piper asked him. The groaning sounded closer. 'I think I do' Thomas said, crawling out of the bush and making his way across a few trees.

Both of them quietly crawled through trees, bushes and many startled insects on their hands and knees. Finally, they came to a clearing. It was a huge lake in the middle of the woods.

The lake sparkled and shimmered in the dark. The water lapping on the grounds. It was beautiful. 'What are we supposed to do?' Piper asked Thomas. 'We'll hide in the lake' Thomas replied.

'Are you crazy?' Piper asked. 'My idea's are much better than your ideas' Thomas replied wryly thinking about the train and how it had ended.

'We have no time to argue' Piper whispered urgently. She took out her fanny pack and hid it in the bushes then she ran over to the lake and stopped abruptly. There was no way she was going to get in with her heels but there wasn't time. She waded in and then ducked.

She had been thought how to hold her breath for long periods of time during training and she put it to use now. She looked around the lake.

She could see muddy sand and seaweed at the bottom. Fishes swam around the two of them with quite a bit of curiosity. Piper felt her clothes clinging to her.

If it was one thing, she hated the most, besides lizards, frogs and cockroaches was getting wet with her clothes on. She pointed to her wrist and then raised her eyebrows asking Thomas how long. He held up two fingers and then went up.

Thomas could see two men, Ken and the hooded figure flying on a surfboard now. Technically, they were just standing on it and the surfboard was flying on its own.

He ducked back into the water, pointed to the top and made an X with his hands. Piper understood and closed her eyes. They would be discovered anytime now.

13

Both of them walked on in silence. 'Um, sorry if I was rude to you in the morning' Thomas said, breaking the silence. Piper stopped. 'Its fine' she said. 'Was that your dad in the picture?' she asked him. She was pretty sure she had crossed the limits with that question when Thomas remained quiet.

'Thomas?' she asked after a pause. 'That was my brother in the picture' Thomas said quietly. 'Oh. What happened to him?' Piper asked slowly. 'Got killed' Thomas said, hiding his face.

'Oh I- I get how it is' Piper said, walking along slowly dragging her feet. 'Its not like your brother was killed' Thomas said. Piper looked at him. It was either now or never. 'I'm not sure whether my brother is alive or not' Piper said to him.

'You have a brother?' Thomas asked, genuinely surprised. 'Actually two brothers and one sister' Piper confirmed. 'Why did you want to get into the scavengers?' Thomas asked. Piper looked at him. 'If I tell you, will you promise not to tell anyone?' she asked him. 'I swear' Thomas said.

Piper narrated the whole story. How her name wasn't Summer Mannering but Piper Herbert. How she and her brother's were spies. She told him about the mission, Mr

Vanhoover, and Charlie. She told him about James, how he was on another mission and had not contacted anyone for over 2 months now.

When she finished, Thomas whistled. 'Whoa' he said, sitting on a tree stump. 'tell me about your story' Piper said. 'When I was eight, my parents passed away suddenly. My brother was over 21 when that happened and he became my legal guardian. Then, one night somebody murdered him' his voice shook. 'How old were you?' Piper asked him.

'I was thirteen then. Anyways, my only relatives left were my aunt and uncle but they were cruel. I ran away from home and Ken found me and took me in. I was very grateful to him for sometime until I discovered that his father had killed my brother' he said 'And from the day I figured that out I wanted revenge' Thomas finished.

'Do you know who Ken's father is?' Piper asked. Thomas shook his head. 'His father worked as a joker in a circus' he said. 'Evan took me there the night he was murdered.'

'That must've been a hard time for you' Piper said. Thomas nodded. Thomas stopped suddenly. 'Follow me' he whispered hoarsely. They made their way out of the woods and down the mountain.

'Why are we going into town?' Piper asked Thomas. 'We have to find Charlie you know' she said stiffly. 'You'll find him' Thomas reassured her. They came to the entrance of town and made their way to the café she and Kate had come the other day.

What are we doing here?!' Piper hissed frantically. They made their way to the back of the shop. There was a window through which they could see what went inside the café.

The front door was locked and bolted but what Piper saw made her stare into the shop. From where they were standing, they could see the interior properly. The chairs and tables were pushed back.

There was a huge piece missing of the black and white patterned floor right in the middle. Around it sat two people. Ken and someone older.

Technically, Ken was sitting and the hooded figure that had chased Piper and Thomas through the woods the other day was standing in front of him. He must've been yelling something. Only if he would remove that cloak.

'Is that Ken's dad?' Piper whispered. She couldn't hide the feeling that she knew the man. 'I'm not sure' Thomas whispered back.

'The person who killed Evan was tall, and wore a golden ring' Thomas said. 'Cant you be more specific?' Piper asked him. 'Tons of people wear gold rings' she said.

'Uh Piper?' Thomas said, looking into the shop. 'We better run' .

14

Piper held her breath underwater as long as possible. She could hear conversations now. It was mostly muffled but she could make out a few sentences.

'Dad it can't be Summer and Thomas' Ken was arguing with the hooded figure. What came after that was muffled. 'I saw them this evening' Ken replied. 'Why, Summer's leg was aching the whole day and Thomas is still in shock about his brother' Ken said firmly.

Thomas balled up his fists under the water. After a few minutes, father and son both turned silent. Piper wasn't sure if they were there or not but she couldn't hold her breath any longer.

She burst out of the water and into the cloudy night. Rain clouds were beginning to gather. She shivered in the cold air. Thomas came up next to her.

'Its pretty cold' Piper said shivering. They got out of the water and Piper shook herself like a dog would. 'My clothes' she said, shaking with the cold. 'They'll dry' Thomas said.

Piper walked back to the bushes to retrieve the fanny pack. 'Do you have anything in the fanny pack?' Thomas asked. Piper shook her head as she clipped it on. 'I do have a couple of tissues and a napkin' she said.

Thomas rolled his eyes. 'As if that's gonna help us' he said. Piper shook herself again. 'We need to find the shack' she urged. 'Ken's doing something dangerous that we don't know about.'

Thomas looked at her. 'There are woods everywhere in like a two hundred miles radius' Thomas explained. 'There is no way we can find the shack tonight' he said. Piper thought for a moment.

'There is one way though' she said slowly, her eyes lighting up. 'What' Thomas asked, exasperated. 'If one of us gets close to Ken, we get the information I want' she said, looking straight at Thomas. He shook his head violently.

'Piper, Ken's only going to share information with you' he said. Piper scowled. 'How are you so sure?' she said scowling. Thomas raised his eyebrows in exasperation. 'Alright' she said after a pause.

'Hey Ken' Piper was saying the next morning when Thomas walked in. 'Hey Summer' Ken said. 'Mind if I sit with you?' Piper asked him. 'Sure' he said.

'So, were you always the leader of the Scavengers?' Piper asked him as they sat down. Ken's face turned dark. 'Three years ago, I was just a member of the gang. Our old leader fell sick all of a sudden. I thought I would get the leadership but then someone else joined the gang. He beat me in a dual but I imprisoned him before he has the chance to spread the news' Ken said, grinning.

'What was his name?' Piper asked, suddenly excited. 'Charlie Herbert' Ken said, his face turning different shades of colours with each passing second.

Piper almost fell down her chair. She searched the crowd for Thomas and spotted him talking to Kate. He caught her eye and she nodded, smiling. Then she turned back to Ken and shook her head.

'You must know more about him, as you know...you imprisoned him' Piper prompted. 'turns out he has three siblings' Ken said laughing out loud. 'Siblings who don't even care' he said roaring with laughter. Piper felt herself turn red with rage. 'How do you say so?' she asked him. 'Isn't it obvious' Ken said. 'They didn't even bother to search for him' he said.

***

Piper couldn't sleep that night. She lay awake on her bed and was just dozing off when something startled her. She got up and slowly crept to the door. Something dark was deftly moving towards the end of the corridor.

She crept out just to see Kate dressed in dark clothes going along the corridor. What was she doing in the middle of the night.

15

Piper ran out of the room and looked around the corridor. She was pretty sure Thomas's room was on the other side. Suddenly Kate stopped and cursed to herself. Piper stood against the wall like a statue.

Kate went back into the room and Piper started running. She reached Thomas's room and started knocking softly. Thomas opened the door on the first knock. His hair was all messed up.

He almost screamed when he saw Piper at the door. Piper held a finger to her mouth and gestured towards the opposite side. Kate was coming back out. Thomas' eyes went wide. 'One sec' he whispered.

He came back out and the two of them ran down the stairs to the huge quadrangle. Kate was swiftly walking towards the huge entrance. The two of them shadowed Kate all the way to the clearing with two tunnels.

Piper could see the train tracks gleaming in the moonlight. Kate took the second tunnel and Piper and Thomas followed. It was a dark tunnel, cobwebs hanging from the ceiling.

Piper stifled a scream when she saw a bat swoop past her. Kate kept walking on, not looking back even once. After walking for what seemed a hundred miles Kate stopped in front of a waterfall.

It was a huge beauty. The water glimmered and glistened in the moonlight as if possessed by magic. The only thing that seemed disturbing was the sight of four crocodiles swarming in the waterfall. Right above the waterfall was an old shack. It was the same one Piper had seen in the picture. Her heart started racing as she clutched Thomas' arm. 'That's it' she whispered urgently. Right next to the shack was a huge tower.

Kate was now climbing huge rocks that led to a landing. Right in front of the landing was a rope. It was hung right below the crocodile infested waters.

The rope had tyres hanging from the top. The tyres were tightly wound and knotted on the main rope. It was like an obstacle course without the safety harness.

Kate swiftly held the rope and kept her foot onto the first tyre. It shook dangerously. Carefully but quickly, she passed all the tyres and landed on the cliff right above the shack.

The shack itself was a very desolate prison. You couldn't cross the tyres and even if you did you would be totally lost. 'C'mon' Thomas whispered, climbing the rocks. Piper quickly shook her head and stepped back.

'I'm not-' Piper started. 'Why?' he asked. She pointed to the alligators and shivered. Thomas looked at them for a minute and then smiled. One alligator had been continuously roaming around the side. Thomas walked towards it and put his hand out.

Piper yelled and dove in front of him. Thomas's hand passed right through the alligator. 'It's a very good fake but realistic alligator' he said grinning.

Piper stood in shock and then followed Thomas to the rocks. She put one of her heels on the tyre and shivered. Slowly, she walked across and landed on the cliff with the help of Thomas.

The door of the shack was ajar and Piper crept towards it. Kate was busy walking around the room, holding something in her hand. Piper recognised it instantly as the cloak the hooded figure had been wearing the whole time. Was Kate the figure who had chased them? Somehow it just didn't feel right.

Kate dropped the cloak and ran to a corner of the shack. A huge cell was shifting into shape from the back. 'Charlie' Piper heard Kate whisper. 'Kate...is that you?' Charlie's voice came back. Kate nodded and frantically worked on the lock.

Charlie lumbered out of the cell and hugged Kate. Both of them talked in hushed tones. Piper thought back to two years. Suddenly she was beginning to recognise Kate.

She remembered the day Charlie was assigned this mission, he had told them that he was going to work with his girl called Kate. Now she understood that this was the Kate he had been talking about. 'How's Piper?' Charlie asked Kate. 'She and Thomas followed me here' Kate said with a smile.

The door opened and Charlie and Kate stepped out. Piper was thunderstruck for a second and then went hurtling towards him. To Thomas' surprise, Kate didn't look a bit surprised to see them.

'You guys are friends?' Thomas asked in awe. He looked at Kate to Charlie. Kate laughed and nodded. 'Kate, you work for spies1991 too?' Piper asked her, still in a daze. Kate grimaced. 'Used to' she said. Before Piper had the time to ask why, the cloudless sky suddenly turned cloudy. 'Uh oh. Something bad is gonna happen' Piper said softly. She reached for the shack and the others followed.

The shack only had two doors one marked entrance and one marked exit, the cell and a couple of old swords and shields hanging from the walls. Piper felt another presence in the room. 'I SEE YOU ALL ARE HERE' a voice suddenly rumbled and Mr Vanhoover landed in front of them.

Her mouth dropped open. 'I-Mr Vanhoover? She asked. Was this some kind of joke? She thought.

The man seemed to read Piper's mind. 'This is not a joke miss Herbert' he said glaring. 'I thought you were with the good guys' Piper asked. 'I was' he said. 'Before your father spoilt my career' he said glaring at the four. Charlie clenched his jaw.

'What did dad do?' Piper asked. She was close to Mr Herbert. 'My original plan was to kill your father' Mr Vanhoover said, and then laughed cruelly.

Thomas and Charlie had to hold Piper back from firing at the man. She tried to shake them off but both boys matched, she was outnumbered. 'WHAT.DID.MY.DAD.DO?' she asked growling.

'Your father and I knew each other since we were kids' Mr Vanhoover said. 'We were best buddies when we were young' he said. 'Then I got chosen by the company your father is the CEO of now' he continued growling.

'Then your father decided to join the company and spoilt my career.' To this statement Piper strained to get her arms free but Thomas and Charlie held on.

If Piper got angry, things could get out of hand easily. The crazy man could kill Piper easily.

'I always believed I was better than your father and I still believe that I am better than your father' he said. 'So, if I couldn't get to him, I could always get my revenge on his children.' He laughed to that.

'Do you know how troubled dad was for two years' Piper asked glaring at him. Mr Vanhoover laughed. 'That is what I wanted' he said grinning. 'But now I may as well send him the corpses of you two' he said smiling pleasantly. Charlie and Thomas loosened their grip on Piper's arms. The girl snatched the dagger from Kate and ran towards Mr Vanhoover but before she could get close to him, she fell back.

The madman laughed. 'Ken was right about you' he said. 'He knew who we were?' Piper asked. 'That is one mystery I gave him to solve' Mr Vanhoover said. 'and he would've solved it by now if he wasn't head over heals over you' he muttered under his breath.

'You got us in this mission just to trap and kill us' Piper concluded, shaking. 'Well, I am not doing any of the killing' Mr Vanhoover said. 'Oh no, my servants are going to do that' he said. As he stepped back and disappeared, an army of robots marched towards them.

16

A WHOLE army of robots marched towards the four. It was a HUGE army. Over hundred robots marched in the front. They were a mixture of jungalee jokers and plain robots. The joker was tall and dressed like a joker. The only thing that was disappointing was he had a proper nose instead of a red one. His eyes glowed green, as if recording them. After the hundred metal robots came one GINORMUS scorpion. And behind the GINORMUS scorpion came another army of robots. The shack was changing from a shack to a long battlefield.

'How are we going to defeat them?' Kate asked. Thomas and Piper scrambled around the room and got swords for themselves. Kate and Charlie unsheathed their daggers.

'Tackle as many as you can' he ordered. Ken's lab was rapidly changing. The back was stretching out revealing a huge long room. The robots were getting close slowly. Each robot held a sword and a shield in their hand.

The army advanced rapidly. 'Stay together' Kate ordered. The four huddled close.

The robots started attacking. Piper's sword touched the first robot and he crumpled to the floor.

Anger swelled inside her. Without knowing, she concentrated on her anger and turned it into energy. Her eyes blazed with some kind of bright light. The sword that she had been gripping suddenly crackled with electricity. Her hands felt numb and suddenly, her feet were not on the floor. She was literally FLYING in the air.

Mr Vanhoover yelled uncertainly on the robots, forgetting that they were machines 'ATTACK, you fools'.

The robots advanced uncertainly. Piper slashed her sword and ten robots at once disintegrated into metal.

The scorpion was closing in now. If they didn't do anything now they would be dead meat.

There was the shack exit on the other end. If they could get out without attracting any attention. Piper thought for a moment. She looked at Charlie, Thomas and Kate.

'Kate, do you know how to deactivate the robots?' she asked Kate excited. 'The room is on the top of the tower, guarded by Ken. But I reckon I'll be able to fight him easily' Kate said reassuring her. Piper took a deep breath. 'Run for that exit there, deactivate the robots and I'll tackle the scorpion' Piper said hurriedly. 'Piper are you crazy?' Charlie asked. 'You can get killed' he said. Piper looked at Thomas.

He nodded sullenly. 'Charlie Is right Piper, you can get killed' he said firmly. 'You guys have to trust me on this' Piper said pleading. 'It's a huge risk but it might just work' she said looking at the three. 'What if-' Thomas' voice cracked. 'At least you'll make it out alive' Piper said softly. She looked at Kate who nodded. 'If we rush might just deactivate the robots in time' Kate said.

Her eyes blazed again as she returned back to normal. 'When I say run, you guys run' she ordered. After she had confirmation, she started towards the scorpion, looking for a way to get inside.

The scorpion was over two times the original elephant. Its red claws snapped open and close. Piper got a quick glimpse of the inside of the claw as it snapped open. The inside was lined with pieces of glass and so was the bottom. The sharp pieces of glass glinted dangerously. The scorpion was made of hard strong metal and controlled by a remote controller.

Piper bit her lip. She could see that shards of glass lined the inside of the hollow tube that led from the claws into the scorpion's body. Next to the claws were another, smaller pair of claws. They were just small enough for her, Piper to squeeze through.

Piper put out that possibility though. The tube that led from the smaller claw to the stomach was not very large. There was no way Piper could pass through it.

The only other way in was the tail, which she would have to climb, find a kind of opening, damage it and get inside the stomach probably.

That would be the best idea, she decided. Anyway, it was worth a shot. Slowly but carefully. Piper made her way to the scorpion. Scorpions usually have weak eyesight but she wasn't so sure about the robotic scorpion. She walked towards the scorpion from the side and slowly stepped on the tail, which was swishing.

'Run' she yelled at the others as she battled with the tail. The tail swished and rolled up and down. Piper lost balance and fell on the back of the scorpion's metal body. Thankfully there weren't any pieces of glass sticking out this time. She got up shaking and slowly started walking towards the middle of the body.

***

Meanwhile Kate rushed up the stairs, her dagger in her hand and came face to face with Ken on the spiral landing. The tower was not a very large one. The electric room was on the top floor. It was a fairly small room. There was a huge window, large enough for someone to fall through. Right under the window was the waterfall.

'Nice surprise bumping into you Kate' Ken said pleasantly. He held a remote controller in his left hand. Kate looked around, her dagger held up in defence. But what mistake she made was to not look up at the ceiling. Ken pressed the only button on his remote controller and a whole sheet of sharp glass fell in Kate.

She was so taken by surprise as the whole thing fell on her head, her dagger fell out of her hand and skittered on the floor, right next to Ken's foot.

Blood trickled from her lips and her eyes had a wild look as she lunged at Ken.

***

Downstairs, Vanhoover landed in front of Charlie. 'Why don't you fight Vanhoover' Charlie growled. 'Yea, why don't you do your own dirty work' Thomas prompted him.

'I'm not wasting my energy on non magic people' Vanhoover said stiffly. 'Your sister, Piper has the diary of the great magician' Vanhoover continued. 'What diary?' asked Charlie. 'Piper has the diary of my ancestor. MINE' Vanhoover yelled. It echoed all around. 'If I give you the diary will you leave us alone?' Charlie asked. 'That's the problem' Vanhoover snarled. 'Only she can open it.' Charlie looked at him as if he had gone nuts. I give an oath that I will kill Piper Herbert one day' Vanhoover said. He was now standing on the edge of a cliff. 'Until then, goodbye' Vanhoover said and disintegrated into metal. 'Is he made of metal or is he human?' Thomas wondered out loud as they looked down at the waterfall.

17

Piper took one step at a time, terrified now. The scorpion moved slowly, shivering with each step. It must've had a feeling that someone was on its back because the tail kept swatting down.

Suddenly Mr Vanhoover appeared. 'Ah Piper, you might as well give up now' he said. 'And let a person like you trouble my dad?' Piper shrieked, sarcasm dripping with every syllable. 'No thanks' she said.

'If your father hadn't competed all the time with me' Me Vanhoover started to say. 'Hold up' Piper said. 'My dad never competed with anyone so it's probably you who did it' she said glaring at him. But something nagged at the back of her mind. Could her dad really do that?

She shook the thought out of her head. That wasn't possible and even if it was, it had happened a long time ago. 'I tried distracting your dad with many things he liked but he ALWAYS came out successful' Mr Vanhoover said sadly.

'I've never met someone so selfish and someone as sadistic as you' she said disgusted. Mr Vanhoover glared at her. 'If I want, I can kill you now' he growled. 'Then why don't you?' Piper asked innocently, batting her eye lashes.

Mr Vanhoover has no comment to that. He disappeared into thin air again, leaving Piper on top of the scorpion that shivered and tried to kill her every few seconds.

She took a deep breath and approached the centre of the scorpion, where the shivering took place the most. She bit her lip and made her way towards the centre slowly.

Unfortunately, metal scorpions are usually controlled by remote controllers. And the remote controllers are usually in the possession of the person who created the scorpions.

She looked around desperately for an entry on the top. Their had to be one somewhere.

Then she spotted one. It wasn't on the rear end but then it wasn't in the middle either. Unfortunately, the tail struck right at the entry. Piper walked as close as she could dare, without the tail hitting her.

She noticed a pattern in the framework. The tail went back up and came down ten seconds later. She had ten seconds to stand between the tail and the end of the tail. But fear stopped her from doing so.

Her mind and body wouldn't budge an inch and the tail was coming down fast. Without thinking she backed away and stared at the hole. She had to stop getting scared.

She bit her lip and ignored the feeling of dread. As soon as the tail went up, she ran. Sometimes the most dangerous place in the world is the most safest.

She looked at the entry. She would just have to squeeze in now. She came as close to the opening as she could dare. She braced herself for the fall.

She held her sword that was no longer electric and waited for the tail to go back up. But the tail didn't budge. It just stood over the opening.

The whole army was closing in now. She had to give it her best shot. She jabbed her sword into the curve of the tail. The scorpion groaned and hissed. The tail lifted up a bit and Piper took her chance.

She squeezed in just as the tail fell down again. She looked around her. She was inside the scorpion all right. She felt herself falling down and realization dawned upon her right then, that she did not have a sword. How was she going to kill the scorpion?

***

Ken rolled and Kate fell on the ground. Every part of her body ached with pain. She got up slowly and looked at Ken who was coming to her with her dagger. Just over one move and she would be dead. Ken was standing right next to the window.

Kate jumped up and kicked Ken on the chest. She did it so fast that he toppled over and fell down into the water. She rushed into the room and opened the door. She fumbled around with everything and then pulled down a lever. The robots had been deactivated.

***

18

Piper fell down in darkness for how long she did not remember. She landed with a crash inside the scorpion. From the dim light, she could see shards of glass everywhere. The ceiling was low and she would have to crawl to just miss the glass.

The chink in the armour was right in the middle, covered with shards of glass. Her sword lay on the other end. The only way to retrieve it was to cross the glass.

She could easily cross the glass if she were standing. She slowly started crawling and came across a piece of glass. She gripped it with her hands and pushed it.

The glass came right out of the floor. Piper grimaced with pain as blood started trickling from her hand. She had to get out alive.

She started doing the same thing with other pieces of glass. Her body was drained out of energy as she grasped her sword. Her hands and clothes were covered with blood.

Her face was greased with dust and her hair was dishevelled. Every part of her body ached with pain. She just wanted to lie down and go to sleep. She wished this were a dream.

Slowly she crawled towards the glass shards and stabbed the sword right in the middle with all the energy she could muster. Her eyes glowed golden and then returned back to normal as the scorpion collapsed.

The entire scorpion disintegrated into dust, exposing Piper to the room again. The robots were standing and staring at her now all of them deactivated. Their mouths in a wide line.

Piper didn't waste a minute. She ran towards the exit as fast as she could which was slow considering her situation. Thankfully Kate had deactivated all the robots, only leaving out the scorpions that were controlled by Vanhoover.

She ran towards the exit and opened the door. The three were waiting for her, Ken tied up in ropes. 'Piper!,' Thomas gave a startled cry as Piper crumpled to the floor, exhausted.

***

Piper dreamt of a workshop located in the heart of the woods. Mr Vanhoover sat in the workshop, busy working on a robot. The workshop itself was lined with different parts of robots. All kinds of tools were strewn all around the room.

The robot that Vanhoover was busy working on was a ditto replica of a sea serpent. It was a long robotic snake, over 15 feet long with really scary eyes.

'You escaped this time Piper' Mr Vanhoover was muttering. 'BUT I WILL KILL YOU ONE DAY, REGARDLESS OF THE LEGEND' he said, so loud, it echoed all around the woods.

Piper got up.

She was sitting on a hospital bed. Her head throbbed. The whole Herbert family apart from James and the exception of Kate and Thomas stood next to the bed. 'I'm alive' Piper said, grinning around. Thomas laughed. After all the embraces were over, Piper got up and noticed Mr and Mrs Herbert hiding something.

'We have a surprise for you' Mrs Herbert said. They moved back to reveal James Herbert. Piper stood open mouthed for a minute. 'Hey' James said slowly. Piper ran up to him hugged him. 'Where were you?' she asked, sobbing. 'Tell you later' James whispered.

***

'What happened to Vanhoover and Ken?' Piper asked. She, James, Thomas, Kate and Charlie were sitting around the living room. James kept glaring at Thomas.

'Vanhoover disappeared. We handed Ken over to the police' Kate replied. 'He won't be back for a long time' Thomas said. Piper wasn't so sure.

That night, as Piper was getting ready for bed, there was a soft knock on the door. 'Come in' she called out. Charlie entered the room and flopped down on the bed. 'It's been a rough couple of days hasnt it?' he asked her. Piper nodded.

'Listen' Charlie said after a pause. 'What is it?' Piper asked. 'While you were fighting the scorpion, Vanhoover told me something wierd' Charlie said. Piper grew tense. 'What did he tell you?' she asked. 'He told me about this diary that belongs to his ancestors, that only you can open it and he also said something about you knowing black magic.'

Piper remained quiet for a moment. Then she got up and walked towards her desk. She took out a huge book from the bookshelf above the desk and opened it. it was hollow inside. She took out another leather diary out of the book. It was the most beautiful book Charlie had ever seen in his entire life.

It was a brown leather book with the heading: "A guide to black magic" written in golden letters. Piper opened the book and read some of the spells. 'Piper, I cant see anything' Charlie said puzzled. Piper looked at him and handed the book. Charlie tried opening it but the book simply did not budge.

'Where did you find the book?' he asked her. 'I found it behind our house in the dumpster when I was five' Piper said. 'I had been playing with James that day and the ball flew and landed in the dumbster. I went out to search for it and found the diary' Piper continued. 'Vanhoover is behind it' Charlie said. Piper nodded. 'He thinks he can read whats written in this thing' Piper said scoffing. 'If I know Vanhoover, he is going to attack soon' Charlie warned her. Piper smiled. 'Atleast he isnt attacking right now' Piper said, keeping the book back.

THE END

About The Author

Meet Aanya, 12 years old, is a grade 8 student, resident of Chennai, India. She is a passionate reader and has her own creative style of expressing her voice and stories. Among her favorite books are "A Wrinkle in Time" and "The Way to Sattin Shore," both of which showcase her love for imaginative storytelling and thought-provoking themes.

She's also passionate about dogs. So passionate, in fact, that she decided to use her writing skills to help stray dogs. The portion of the royalties she will earn would go towards helping dogs find a loving home. Her goal is to create a world where all dogs are cared for and loved by their owners.

Aanya loves travelling and is a keen observer. Her sense of adventure extends to her love of travel, which allows her to experience different cultures and broaden her horizons. She also loves to sing and likes to learn many languages.

With a fine eye for details she is very excited to author her first book and will not keep the readers too long waiting to share the other side of this thrilling plot.

Printed by Libri Plureos GmbH in Hamburg,
Germany